# Mr. Putter & Tabby
# Spill the Beans

CYNTHIA RYLANT

# Mr. Putter & Tabby Spill the Beans

Illustrated by

ARTHUR HOWARD

🦤 sandpiper

Houghton Mifflin Harcourt

*Boston   New York*

*For my good friends and neighbors:*
*Riley, Mac, and Dutton*
*—C.R.*

Text copyright © 2009 by Cynthia Rylant
Illustrations copyright © 2009 by Arthur Howard

www.hmhbooks.com

The Library of Congress has cataloged the hardcover edition as follows:
Rylant, Cynthia.
Mr. Putter & Tabby spill the beans / Cynthia Rylant;
illustrated by Arthur Howard.
p. cm.
Summary: Although he would rather be sipping an ice cream soda,
Mr. Putter and his cat, Tabby, attend a cooking class with Mrs. Teaberry and
her dog, Zeke, where they learn one hundred ways to cook beans.
[1. Neighbors—Fiction. 2. Old age—Fiction. 3. Cookery—Fiction. 4. Cats—
Fiction.] I. Howard, Arthur, ill. II. Title. III. Title: Mister Putter & Tabby
spill the beans.
IV. Title: Mr. Putter and Tabby spill the beans.
PZ7.R982Mubp 2009
[E]—dc22 2008005634
ISBN: 978-015-205070-2 hardcover
ISBN: 978-0-547-41433-1 paperback

Manufactured in China

LEO 10 9 8 7 6 5 4 3 2

4 5 0 0 2 8 8 1 6 9

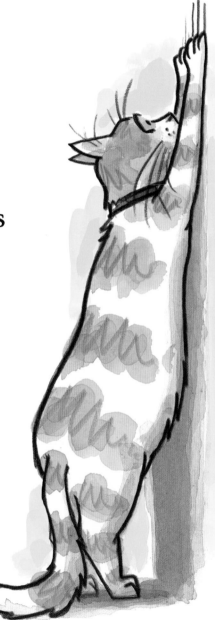

# 1

# Neighbors

Mr. Putter and his fine cat, Tabby,
lived next door to Mrs. Teaberry
and her good dog, Zeke.
They were all good friends and neighbors.
They liked doing things together.
They took long walks.
They had tea.

And sometimes they tried new things.
The new things sometimes worked out.
And sometimes they didn't.
But every new thing
was an adventure.

# 2

# New and Fun

One day Mrs. Teaberry called Mr. Putter
and said she had an idea for
something new to try.
"Something new and fun,"
she told him.

Mr. Putter was trying to
fix his faucet.
It was drippy.
When Tabby tried to sleep
in the sink, the water
dripped on her head.
"I hope the new and fun thing
fixes faucets," said Mr. Putter.

"Oh, it's more fun than that,"
said Mrs. Teaberry.
"It is a cooking class."

"A cooking class?"
asked Mr. Putter.
A cooking class did not
sound like something
new and fun to him.
"Are you sure about
the fun part?"
asked Mr. Putter.

"Of course!" said Mrs. Teaberry.
"Trust me."

When he hung up the phone,
Mr. Putter thought about the many times
he had trusted Mrs. Teaberry.

"I'm still not sure about the fun part,"
he told Tabby.
Tabby just purred.
The faucet wasn't drippy anymore.
She could nap until things
became new and fun.

# 3

# One Hundred Ways

Mr. Putter and Tabby drove to the cooking
class with Mrs. Teaberry and Zeke.
"Are you sure the class is only beans?"
asked Mr. Putter.
"Yes," said Mrs. Teaberry.
"We are going to learn
one hundred ways
to cook them."

Mr. Putter looked at Tabby.
He did not want to learn
one hundred ways to cook beans.
What he wanted was an ice cream soda.

He wanted an ice cream soda with
strawberry ice cream and a cherry on top.
He did not want beans.
He did not want one hundred ways
to cook them.

But he wanted to make Mrs. Teaberry happy.

And sometimes their new things worked out.

When they had gone to the hair show,

he'd won a case of shampoo

that made a very good doorstop.

And when they had gone to the bug festival,

he'd seen a whole new side of Tabby.

Mr. Putter would make the best of beans.

# 4

# Beans

The cooking class had many students.
Mr. Putter and Mrs. Teaberry were the
only ones who brought pets.

The teacher said Tabby
and Zeke were welcome.
But they had to stay
under the table.

BEANS

Mr. Putter did not think Zeke
could stay anywhere
longer than two minutes.
But he didn't tell the teacher that.

He also didn't tell the teacher
that he wanted an ice cream soda.
He told himself to think about beans.
Only beans.
Beans.

# 5

# Granola

When the teacher showed the class
the first way to cook beans,
Mr. Putter was wide awake,

Tabby was purring,
Zeke was scratching,
and Mrs. Teaberry was taking notes.

When the teacher
showed the class
the seventh way
to cook beans,
Mr. Putter was yawning,
Tabby was purring,
Zeke was sniffing,
and Mrs. Teaberry
was taking notes.

*Lima bean gingersnaps*

And when the teacher
showed the class
the fourteenth way
to cook beans,
Mr. Putter was snoring,
Tabby was snoring,
Zeke was chewing
on somebody's granola bar,
and Mrs. Teaberry
was taking notes.

3 bean
jello

Then the woman who owned the granola bar
that Zeke was chewing on
decided she needed a snack.
She reached under the table
to put her hand in her purse.
But her hand did not go into her purse.
Her hand went into Zeke's
sloppy, crunchy, gooey, wet mouth
full of granola.

The woman screamed.

Zeke barked.

Everybody jumped.

The table tipped.

And beans started flying.

# 6
# Wide Awake

It takes a lot of beans to teach a class about
one hundred ways to cook them.
And it is amazing where beans can land
once they start flying.
All of a sudden, Mr. Putter and Tabby
were wide awake,
Mrs. Teaberry had stopped taking notes,
Zeke was eating the first and the seventh
ways to cook beans,
and the teacher had fainted.

It looked as if this was going to be
one of those new things that
didn't *quite* work out.

# 7
## Sodas

At the ice cream parlor,
Mrs. Teaberry helped Mr. Putter
pick beans out of his collar.
Mr. Putter helped Mrs. Teaberry
pour beans out of her purse.
And Tabby and Zeke helped each other
with a banana split.

"At least I learned fourteen ways
to cook beans," said Mrs. Teaberry.
"And I learned how to sleep standing up,"
said Mr. Putter.

They both took a sip from their ice cream sodas.
They both looked at Tabby and Zeke.
"And they stayed under the table,"
said Mr. Putter.
"Yes," said Mrs. Teaberry,
"at least while it was still standing!"

The illustrations in this book were done in pencil,
watercolor, and gouache on 250-gram cotton rag paper.
The display type was set in Minya Nouvelle, Agenda, and Artcraft.
The text type was set in Berkeley Old Style Book.